GRAPHIC MYTHICAL CREATURES

WEREWOLVES

BY GARY JEFFREY

ILLUSTRATED BY GARY JEFFREY AND ROB SHONE

Please visit our website, www.garethstevens.com.
For a free color catalog of all our high-quality books,
call toll free 1-800-542-2595 or fax 1-877-542-2596.

Library of Congress Cataloging-in-Publication Data

Jeffrey, Gary.
Werewolves / Gary Jeffrey.
p. cm. — (Graphic mythical creatures)
Includes index.
ISBN 978-1-4339-6051-2 (pbk.)
ISBN 978-1-4339-6052-9 (6-pack)
ISBN 978-1-4339-6049-9 (library binding)
1. Werewolves—Juvenile literature. I. Title.
GR830.W4J43 2011
398.24'54—dc22
2011004541

First Edition

Published in 2012 by
Gareth Stevens Publishing
111 East 14th Street, Suite 349
New York, NY 10003

Designed by David West Books
Editor: Ronne Randall

Printed in China

CPSIA compliance information: Batch #DS11GS: For further information contact Gareth Stevens, New York, New York at 1-800-542-2595.

CONTENTS

Tooth and Claw

Werewolves are the most ferocious of all mythical creatures. A shape-shifter—half human and half beast—the werewolf has incredible strength, amazing endurance, and great cunning.

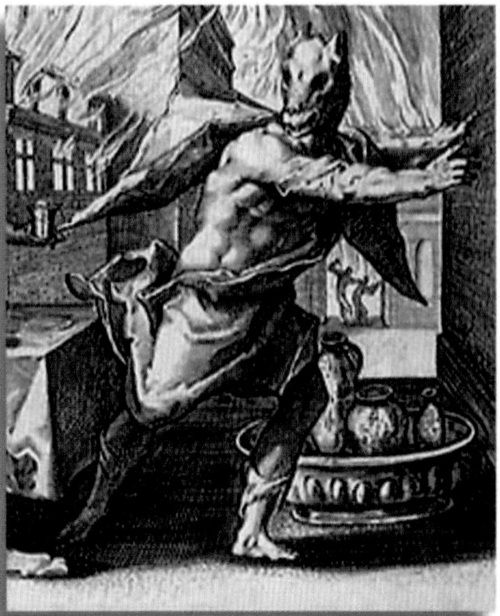

The curse of King Lycaon of ancient Greece is the first recorded myth of a man being turned into a wolf.

Becoming a Werewolf

Traditionally, werewolves were made by a witch's curse. Other ways included being born under a full moon or drinking from the water in a wolf's footprint. It was thought wearing a belt of wolf's fur could also turn you into a rampaging werewolf.

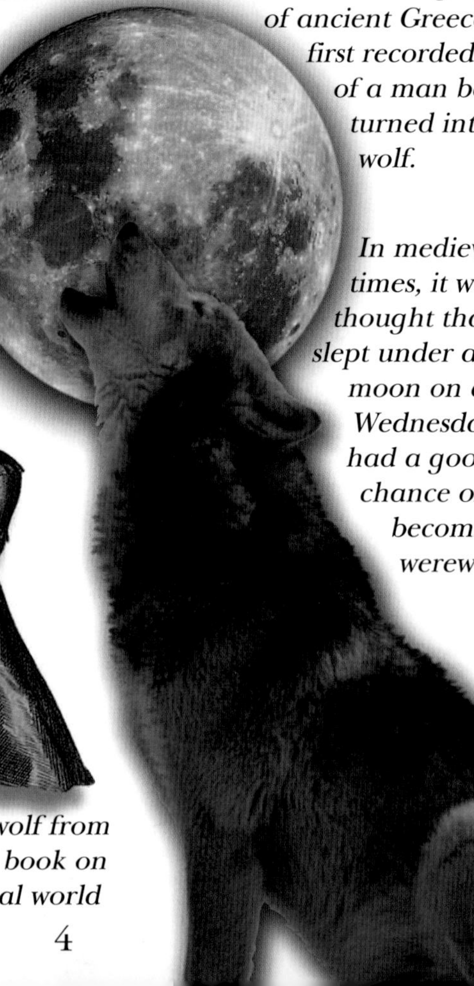

In medieval times, it was thought that if you slept under a full moon on a Wednesday, you had a good chance of becoming a werewolf.

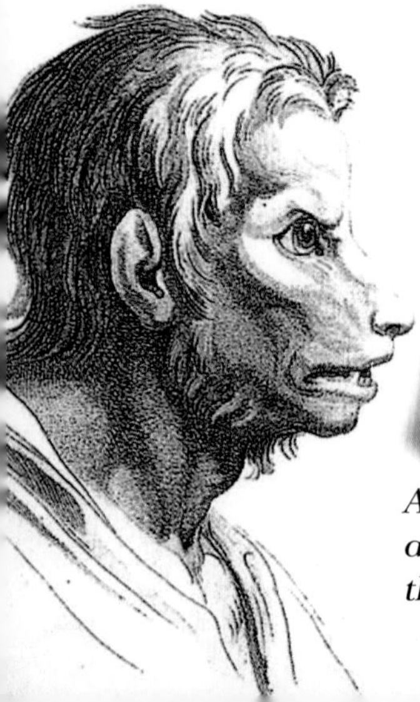

A 19th-century engraving of a man changing into a wolf

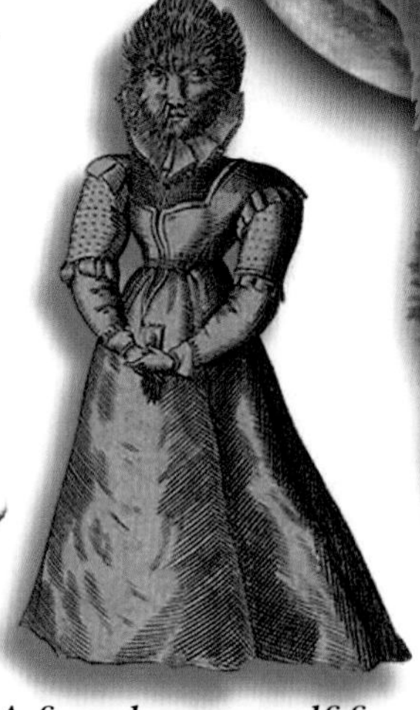

A female werewolf from a 17th-century book on the supernatural world

Haunted by Werewolves

Most werewolf stories come from northern Europe. As medieval settlers made homes in the wild forests, they pushed into the wolves' territory. In hard winters, the wolves would be driven to take domestic animals, or even children, for food. The horror of these incidents gave rise to the cult of the supernatural wolf.

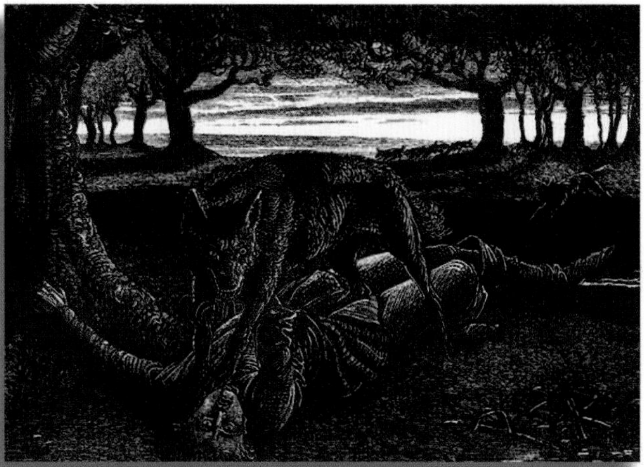

Wolf attacks were usually short and savage.

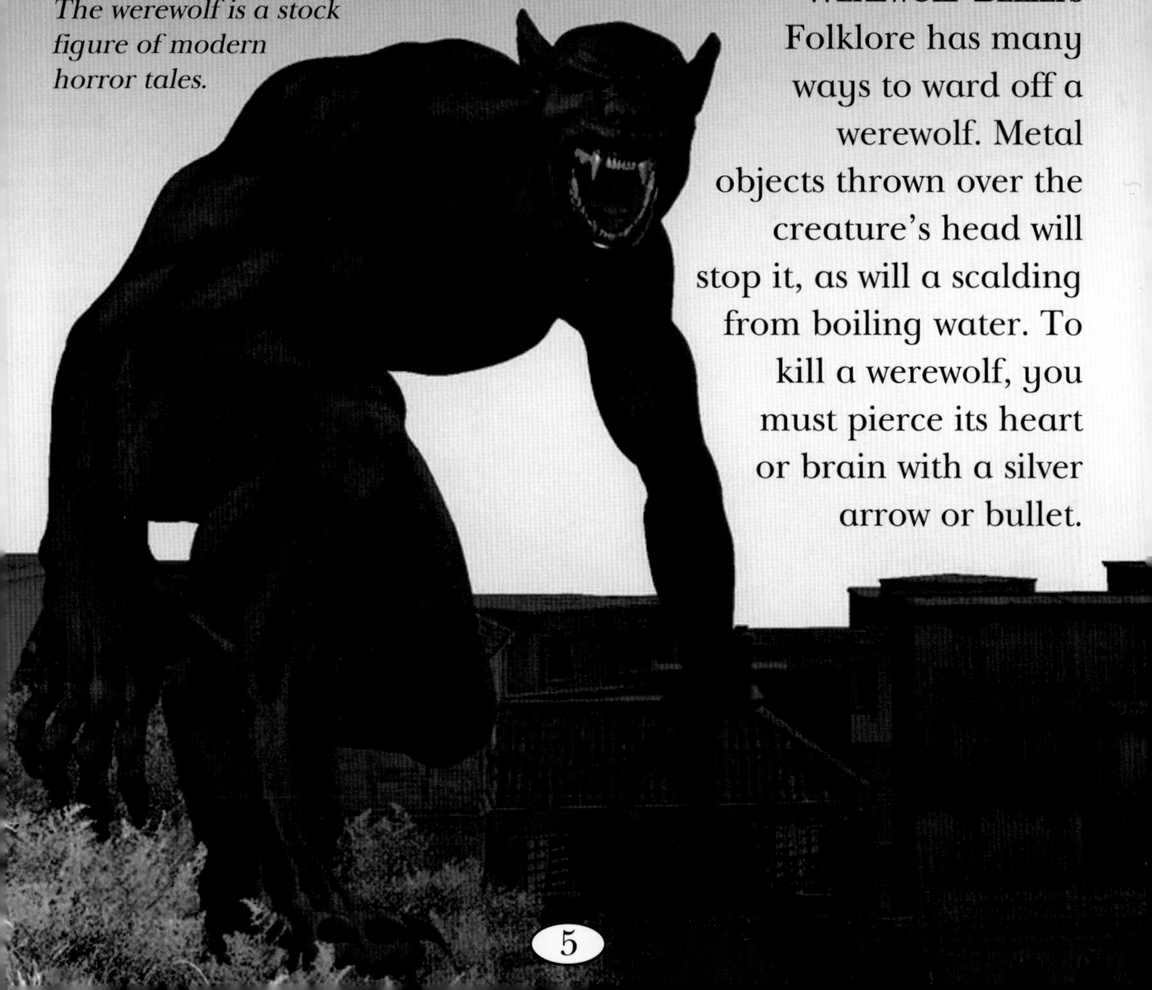

The werewolf is a stock figure of modern horror tales.

Werewolf Beliefs

Folklore has many ways to ward off a werewolf. Metal objects thrown over the creature's head will stop it, as will a scalding from boiling water. To kill a werewolf, you must pierce its heart or brain with a silver arrow or bullet.

The Werewolf of Klein-Krams

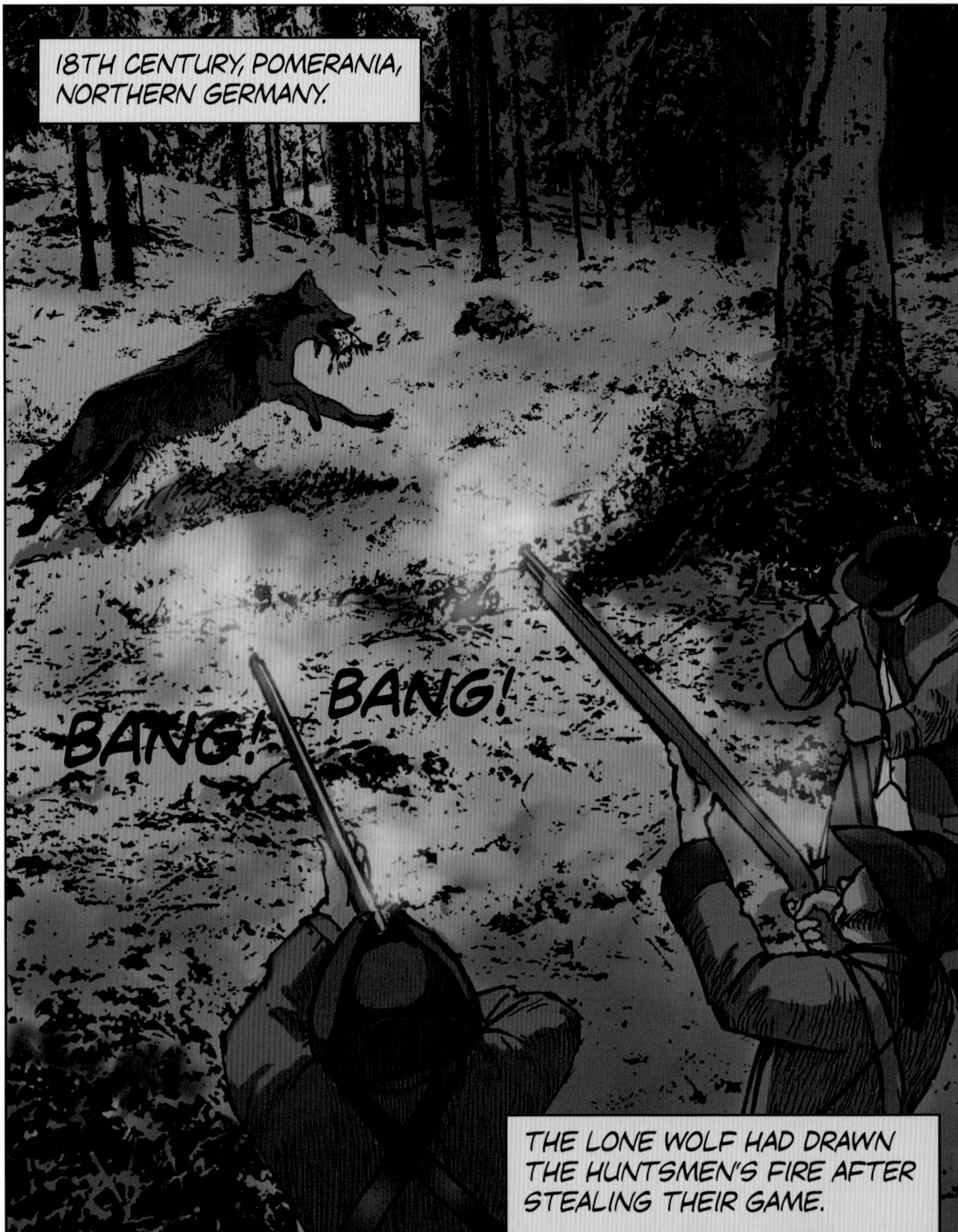
18TH CENTURY, POMERANIA, NORTHERN GERMANY.
BANG!
BANG!
THE LONE WOLF HAD DRAWN THE HUNTSMEN'S FIRE AFTER STEALING THEIR GAME.

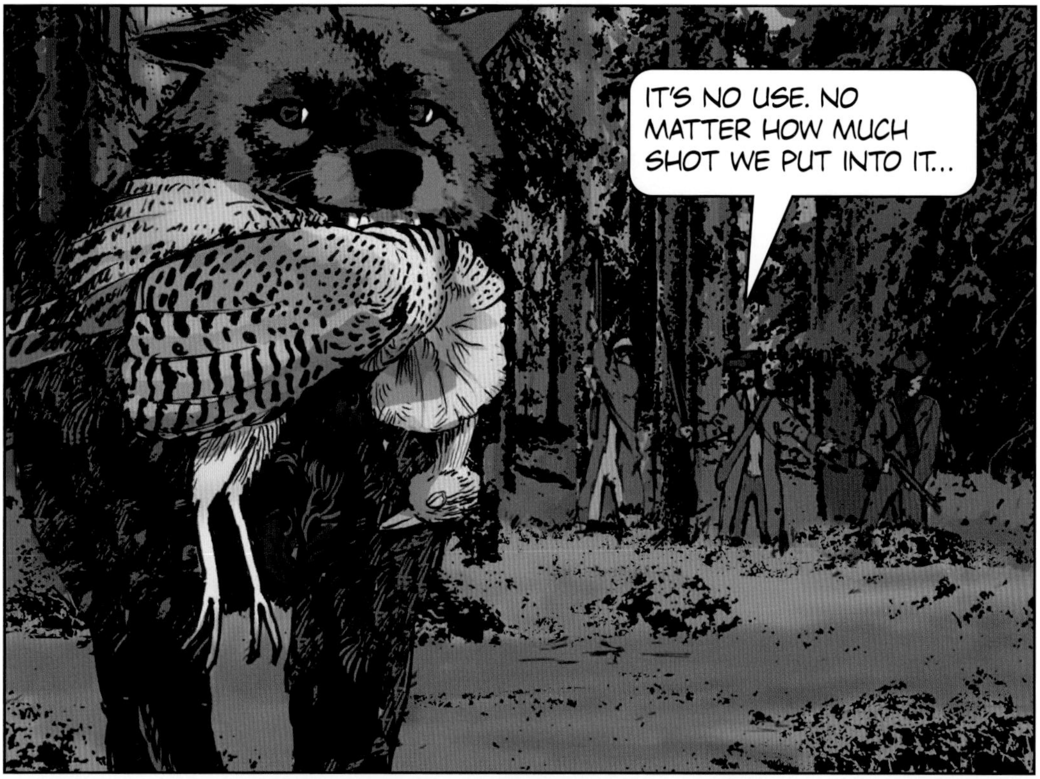
IT'S NO USE. NO MATTER HOW MUCH SHOT WE PUT INTO IT...

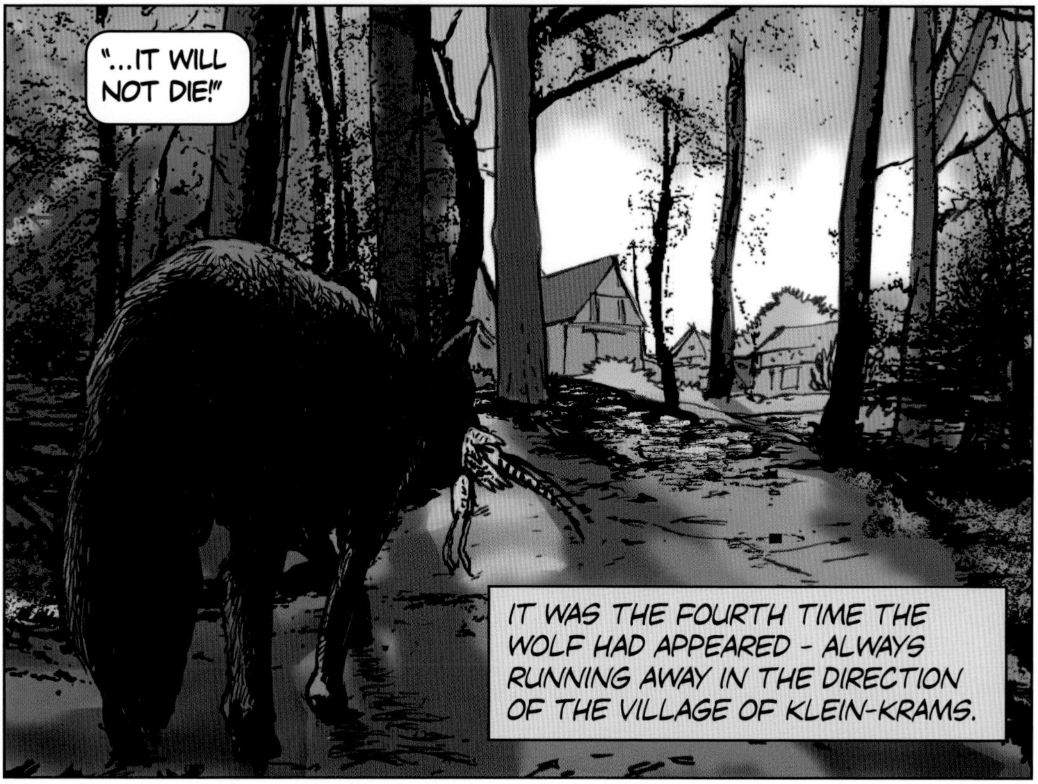
"...IT WILL NOT DIE!"
IT WAS THE FOURTH TIME THE WOLF HAD APPEARED - ALWAYS RUNNING AWAY IN THE DIRECTION OF THE VILLAGE OF KLEIN-KRAMS.

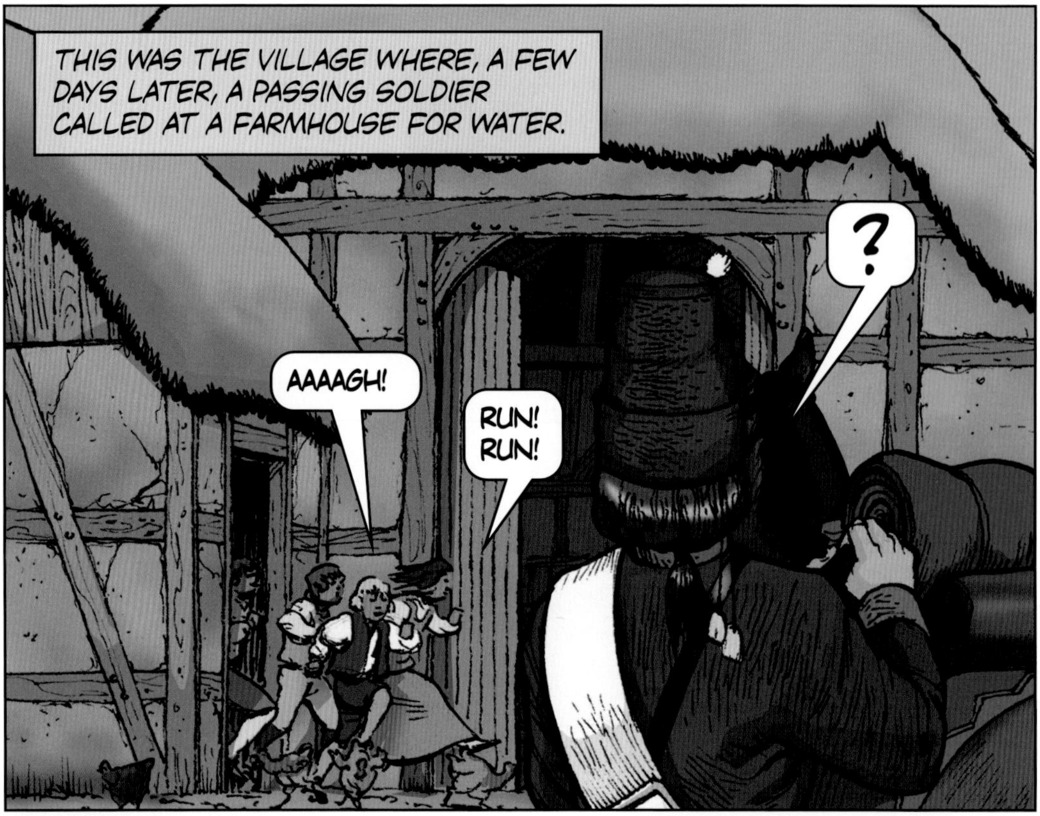
THIS WAS THE VILLAGE WHERE, A FEW DAYS LATER, A PASSING SOLDIER CALLED AT A FARMHOUSE FOR WATER.
AAAAGH!
RUN! RUN!
?

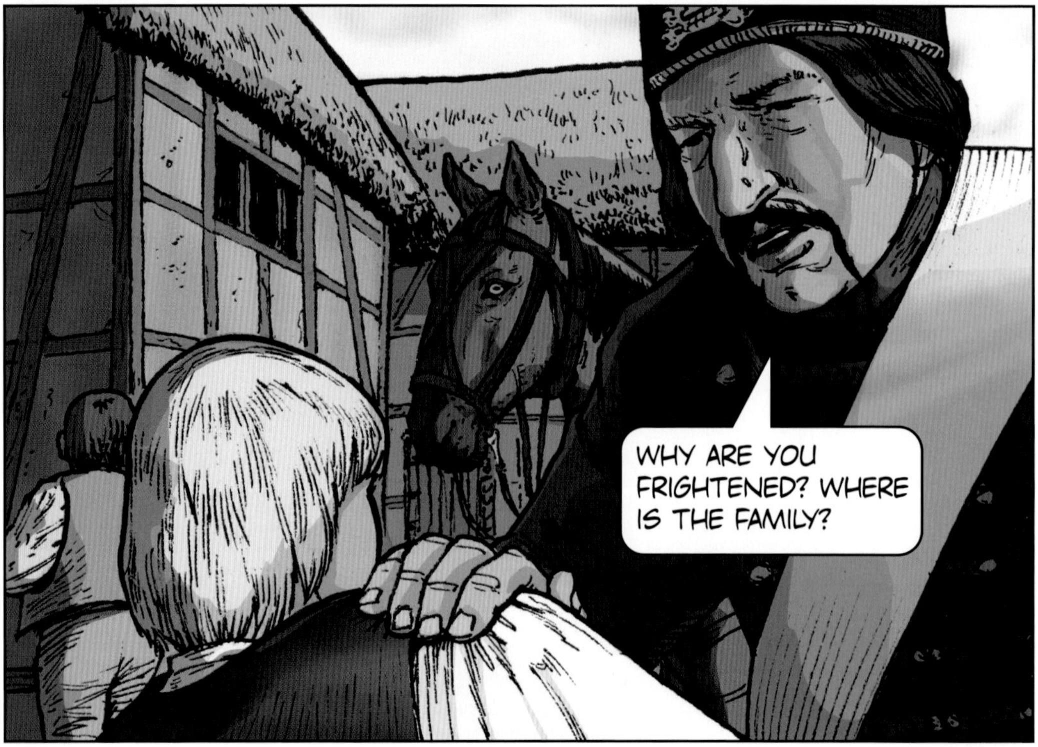
WHY ARE YOU FRIGHTENED? WHERE IS THE FAMILY?

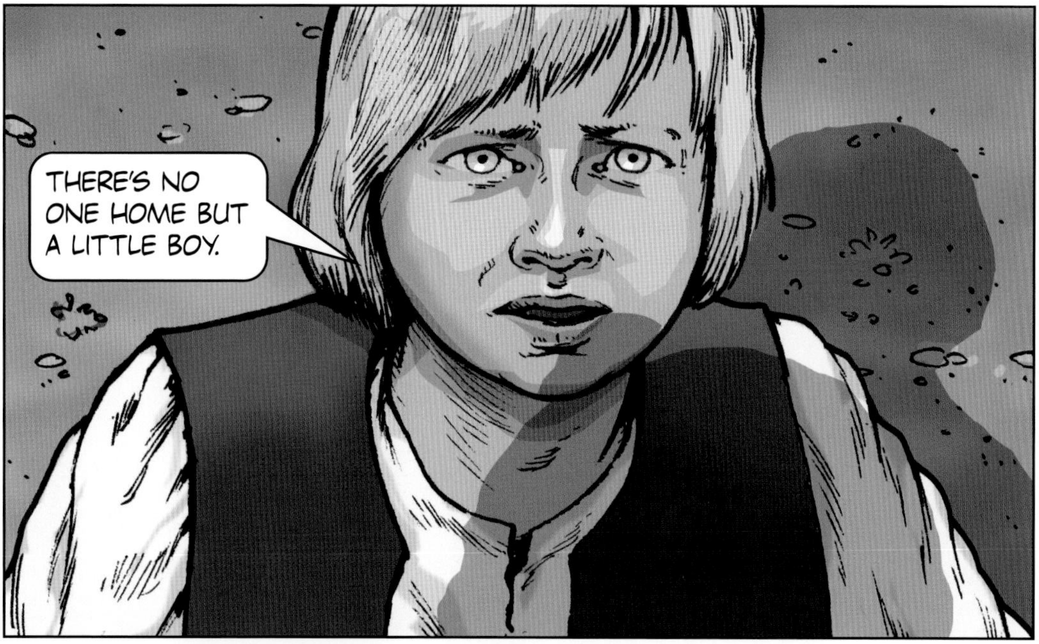
THERE'S NO ONE HOME BUT A LITTLE BOY.

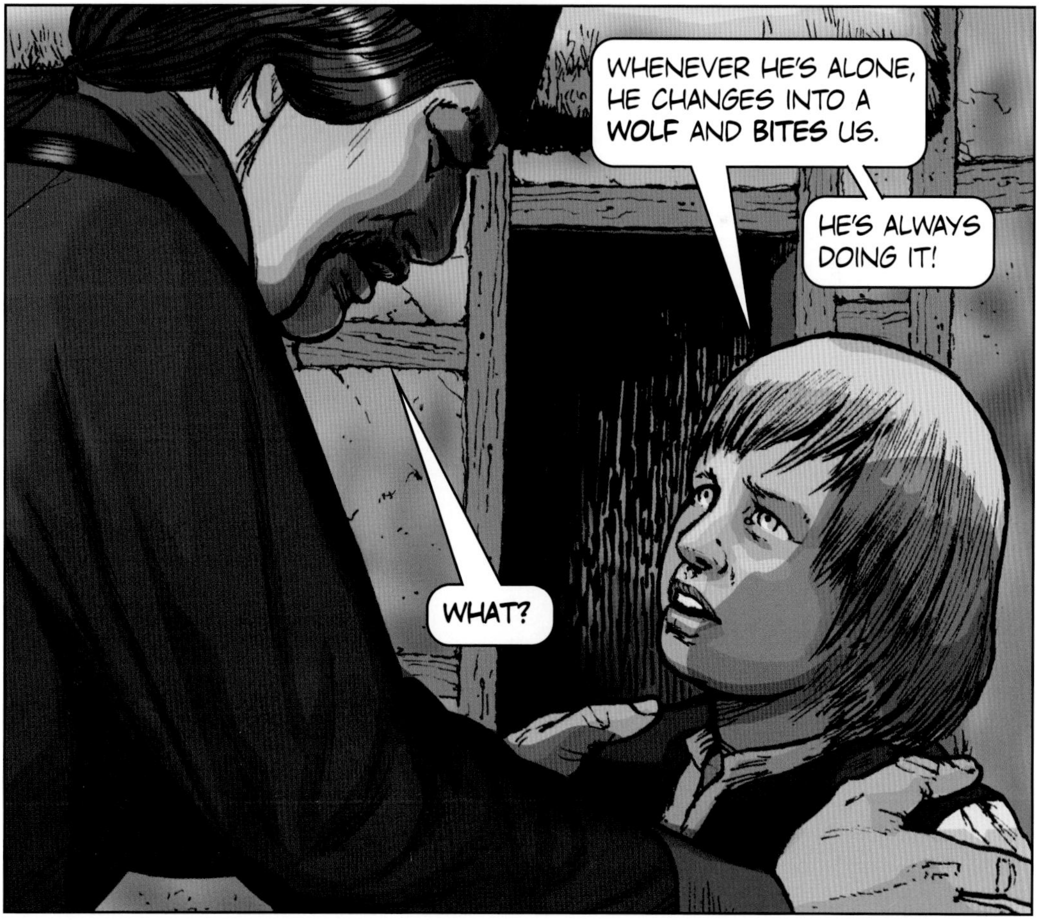
WHENEVER HE'S ALONE, HE CHANGES INTO A WOLF AND BITES US.
HE'S ALWAYS DOING IT!
WHAT?

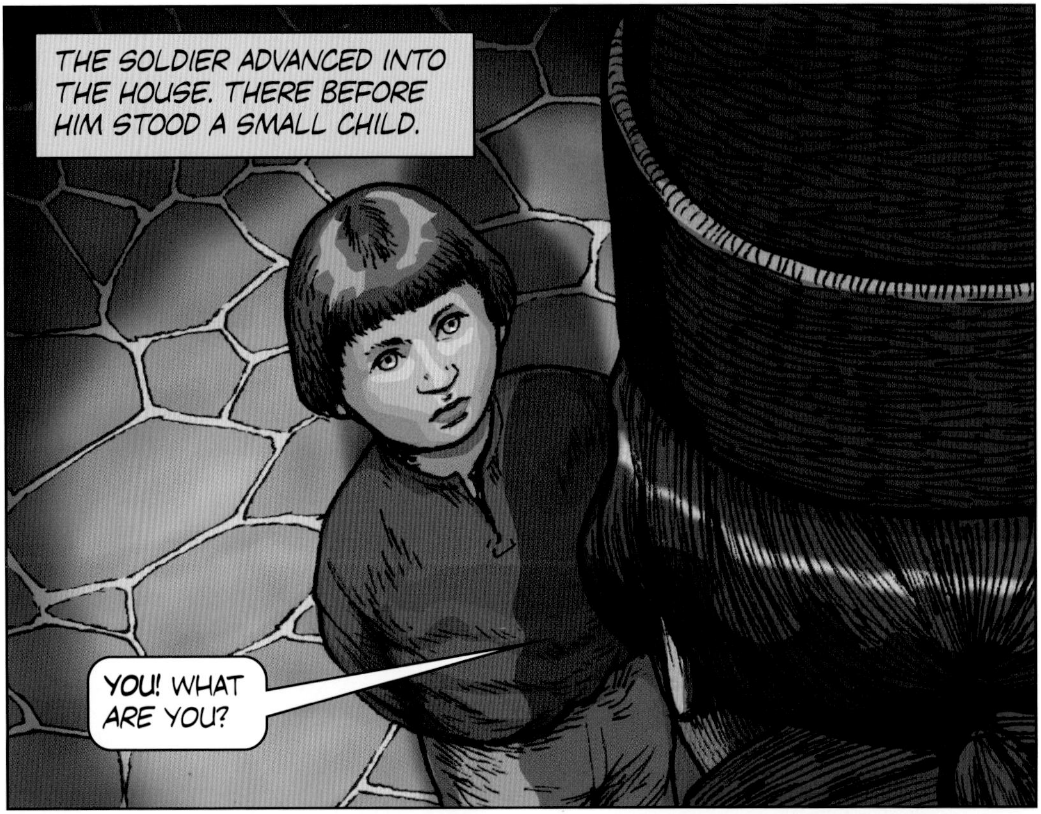
THE SOLDIER ADVANCED INTO THE HOUSE. THERE BEFORE HIM STOOD A SMALL CHILD.
YOU! WHAT ARE YOU?

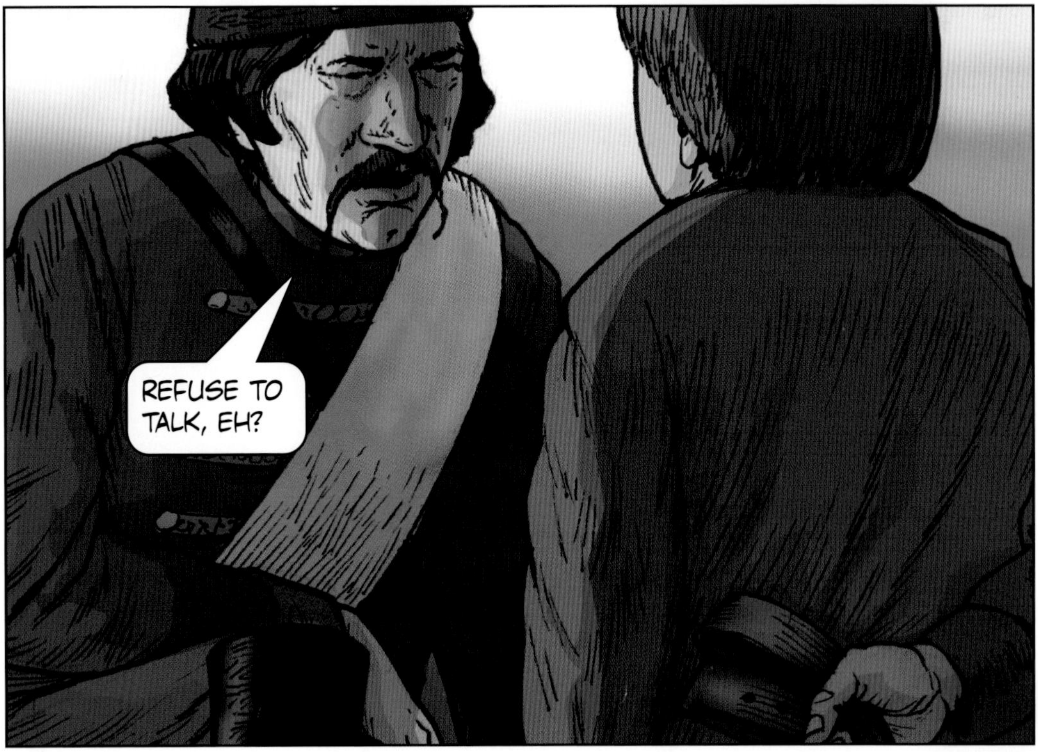
REFUSE TO TALK, EH?

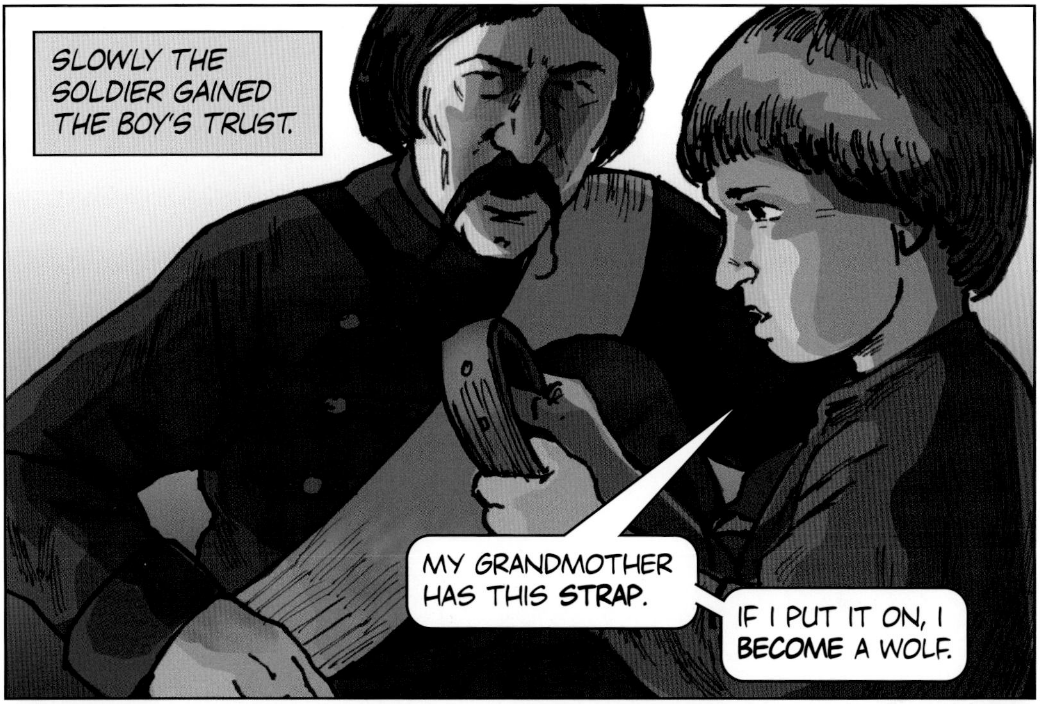
SLOWLY THE SOLDIER GAINED THE BOY'S TRUST.
MY GRANDMOTHER HAS THIS **STRAP**.
IF I PUT IT ON, I **BECOME** A WOLF.

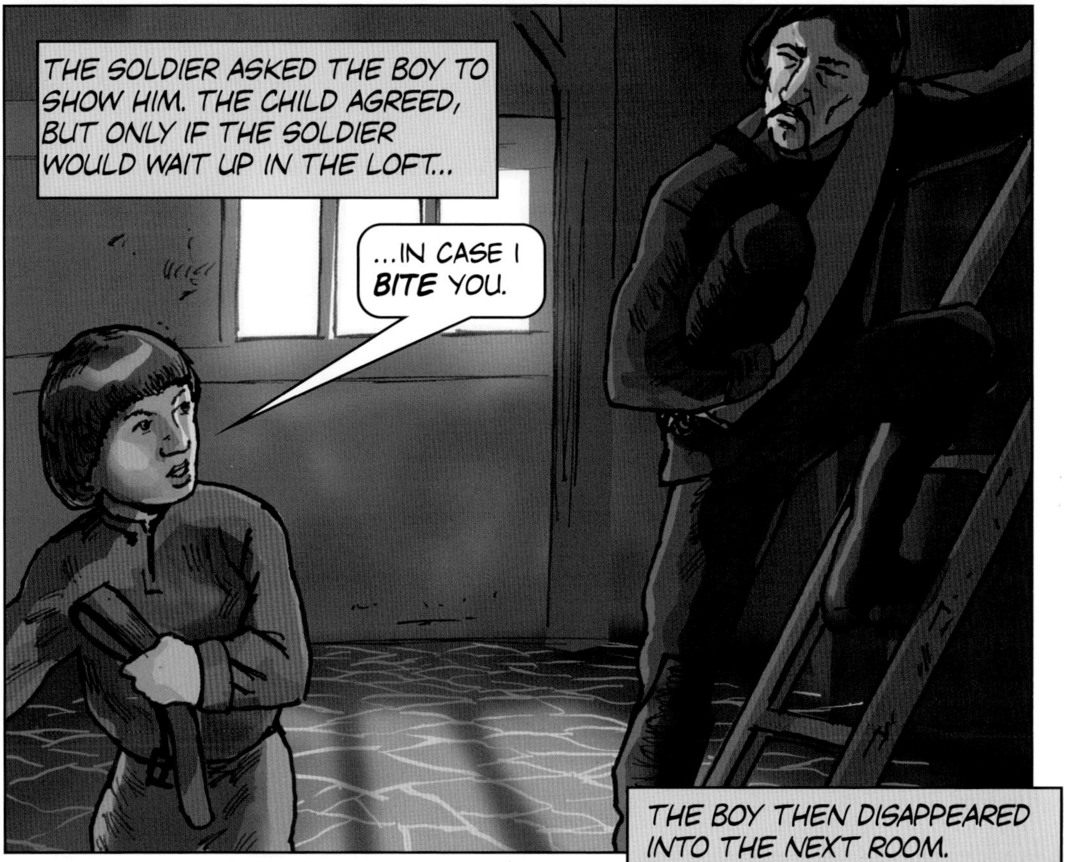
THE SOLDIER ASKED THE BOY TO SHOW HIM. THE CHILD AGREED, BUT ONLY IF THE SOLDIER WOULD WAIT UP IN THE LOFT...
...IN CASE I ***BITE*** YOU.
THE BOY THEN DISAPPEARED INTO THE NEXT ROOM.

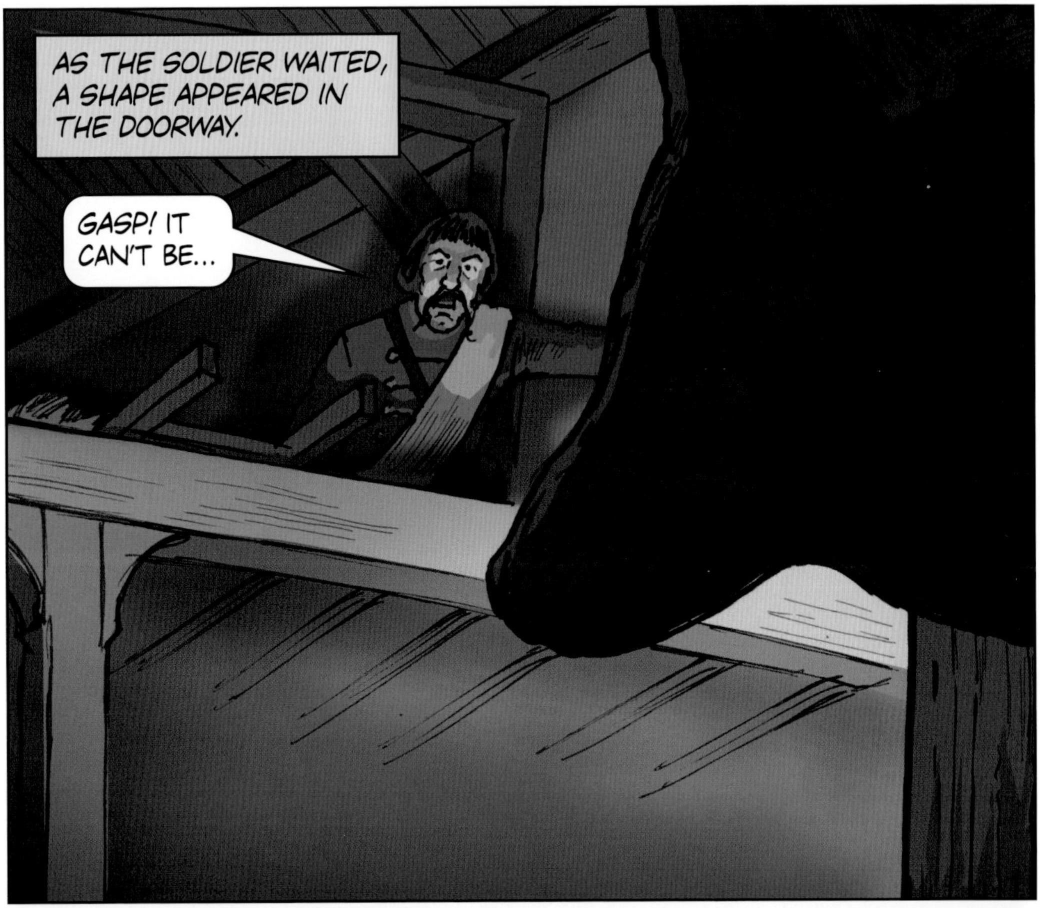
AS THE SOLDIER WAITED, A SHAPE APPEARED IN THE DOORWAY.
GASP! IT CAN'T BE...

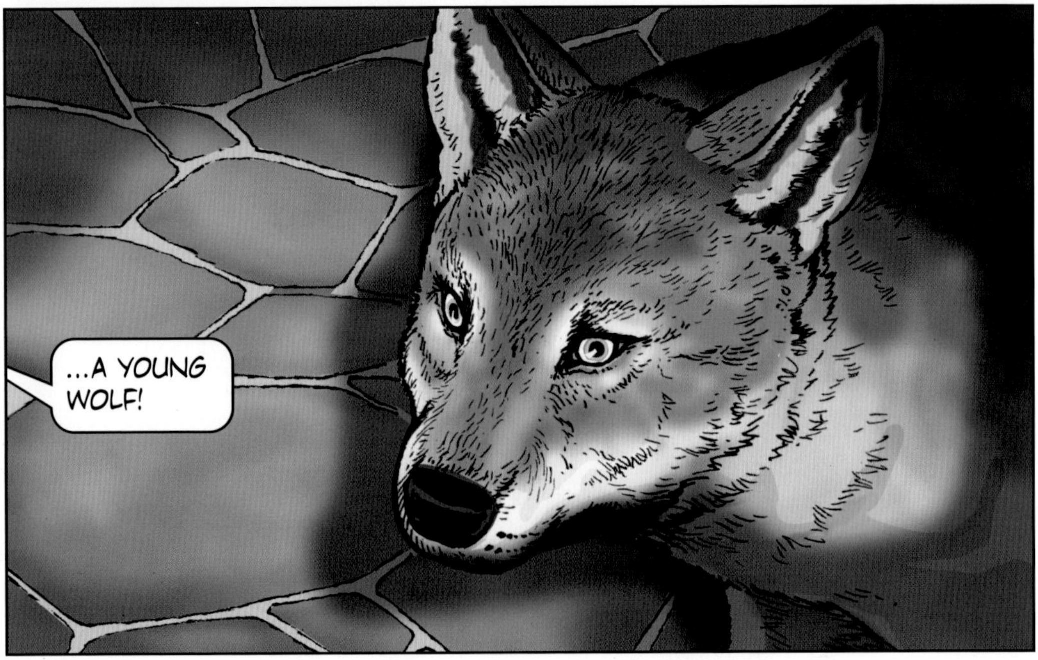
...A YOUNG WOLF!

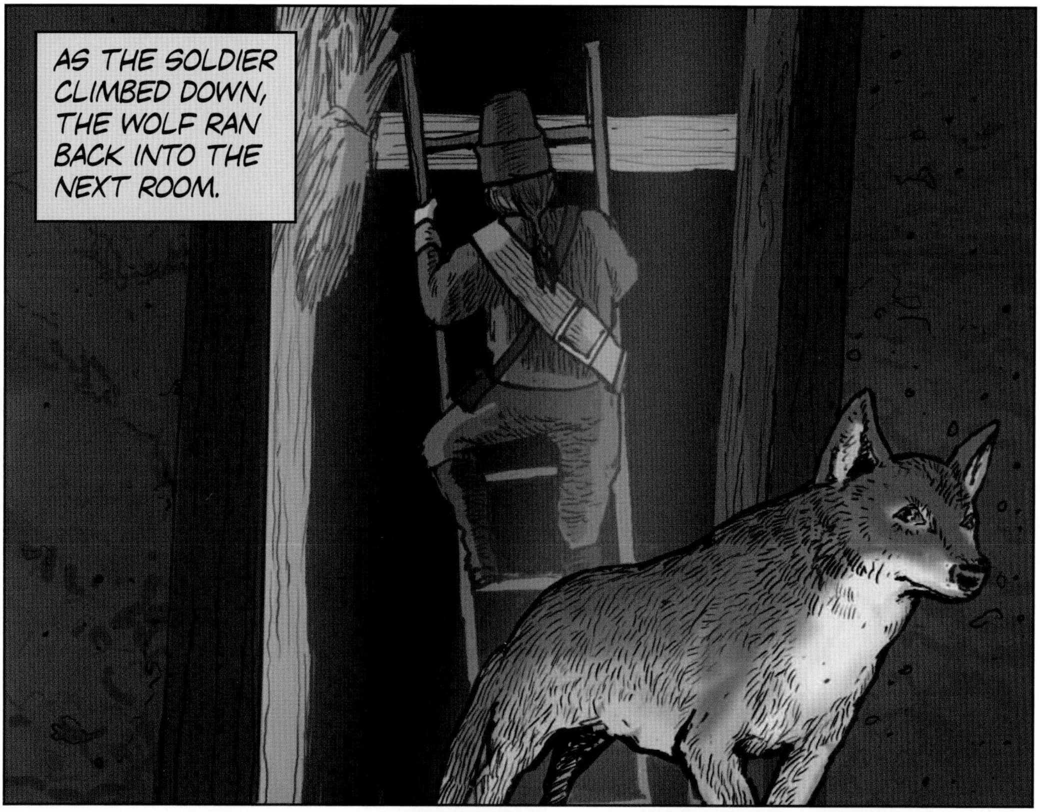
AS THE SOLDIER CLIMBED DOWN, THE WOLF RAN BACK INTO THE NEXT ROOM.

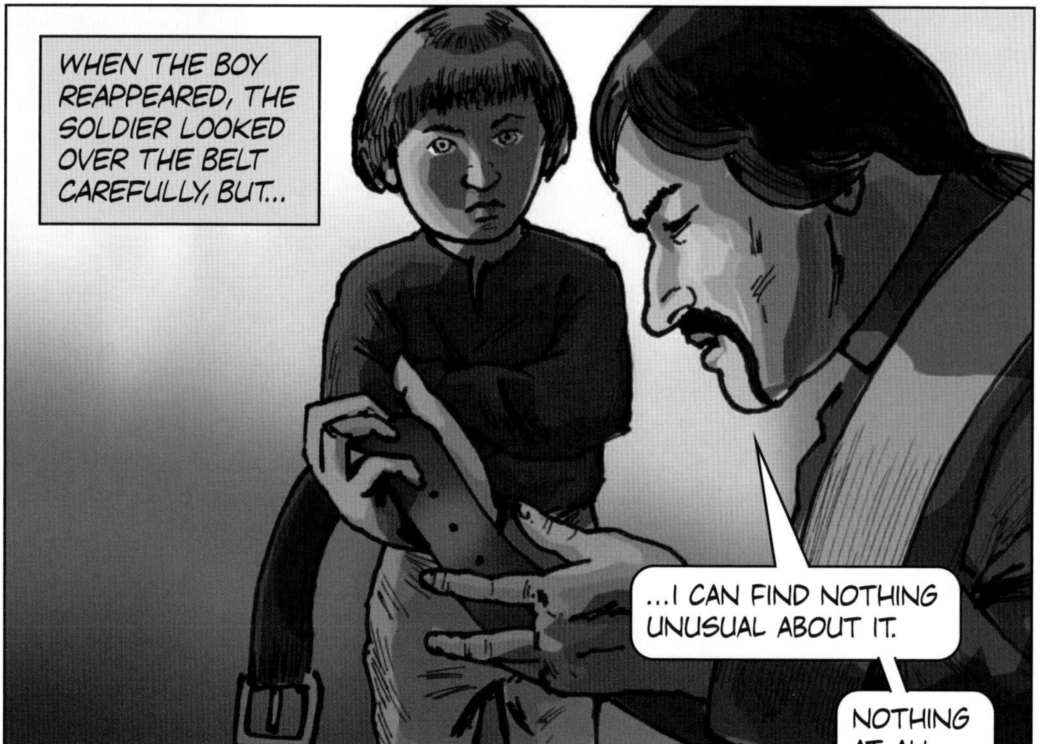
WHEN THE BOY REAPPEARED, THE SOLDIER LOOKED OVER THE BELT CAREFULLY, BUT...
...I CAN FIND NOTHING UNUSUAL ABOUT IT.
NOTHING AT ALL.

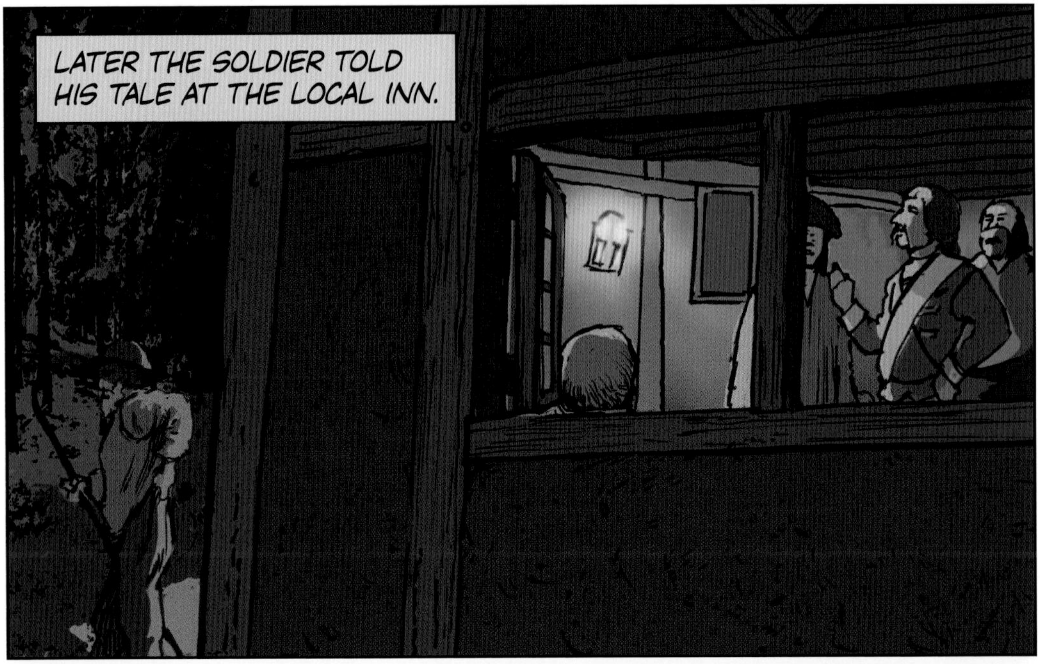
LATER THE SOLDIER TOLD HIS TALE AT THE LOCAL INN.

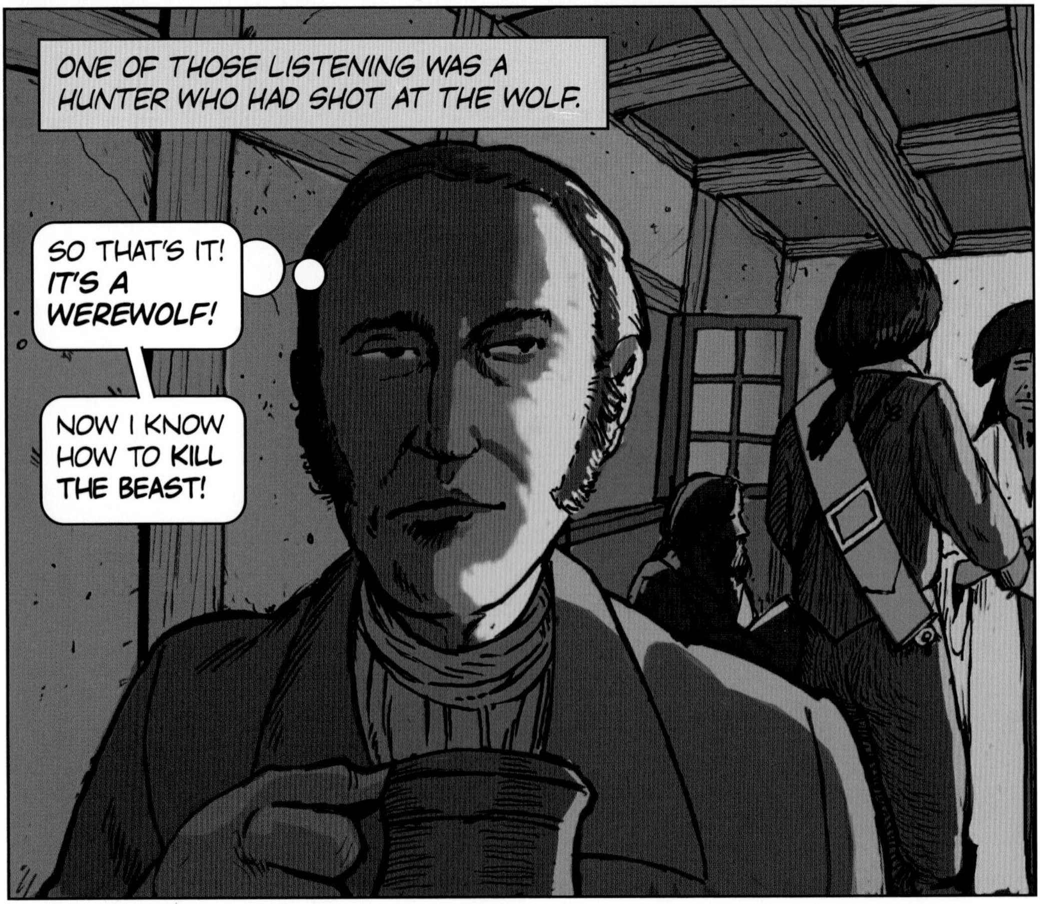
ONE OF THOSE LISTENING WAS A HUNTER WHO HAD SHOT AT THE WOLF.
SO THAT'S IT! IT'S A WEREWOLF!
NOW I KNOW HOW TO KILL THE BEAST!

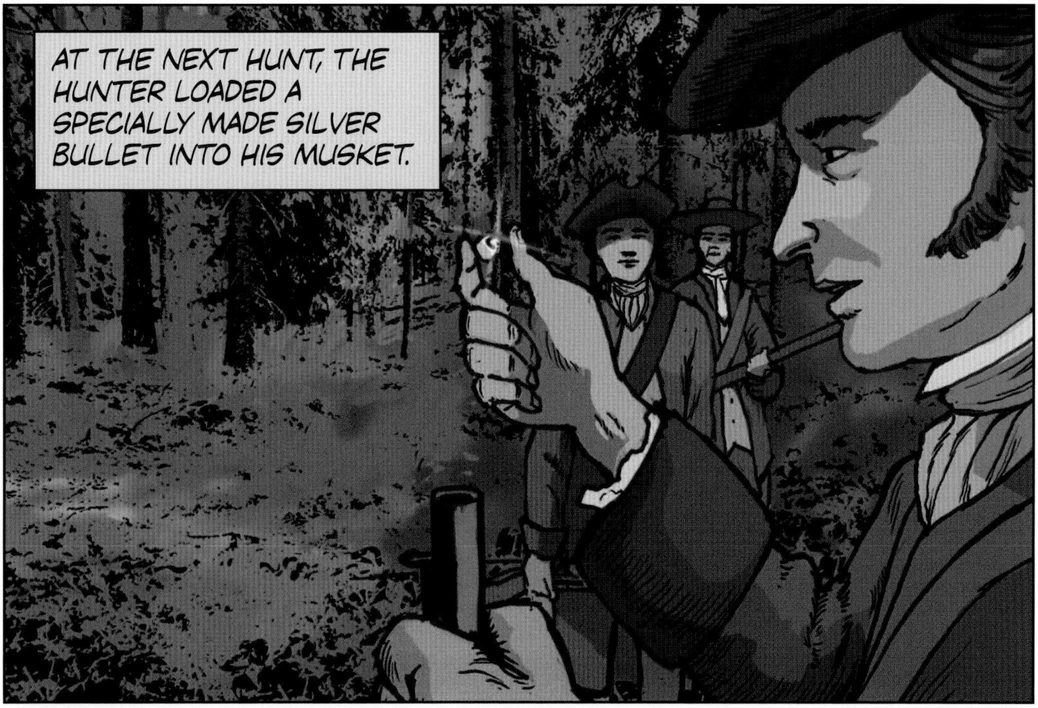
AT THE NEXT HUNT, THE HUNTER LOADED A SPECIALLY MADE SILVER BULLET INTO HIS MUSKET.

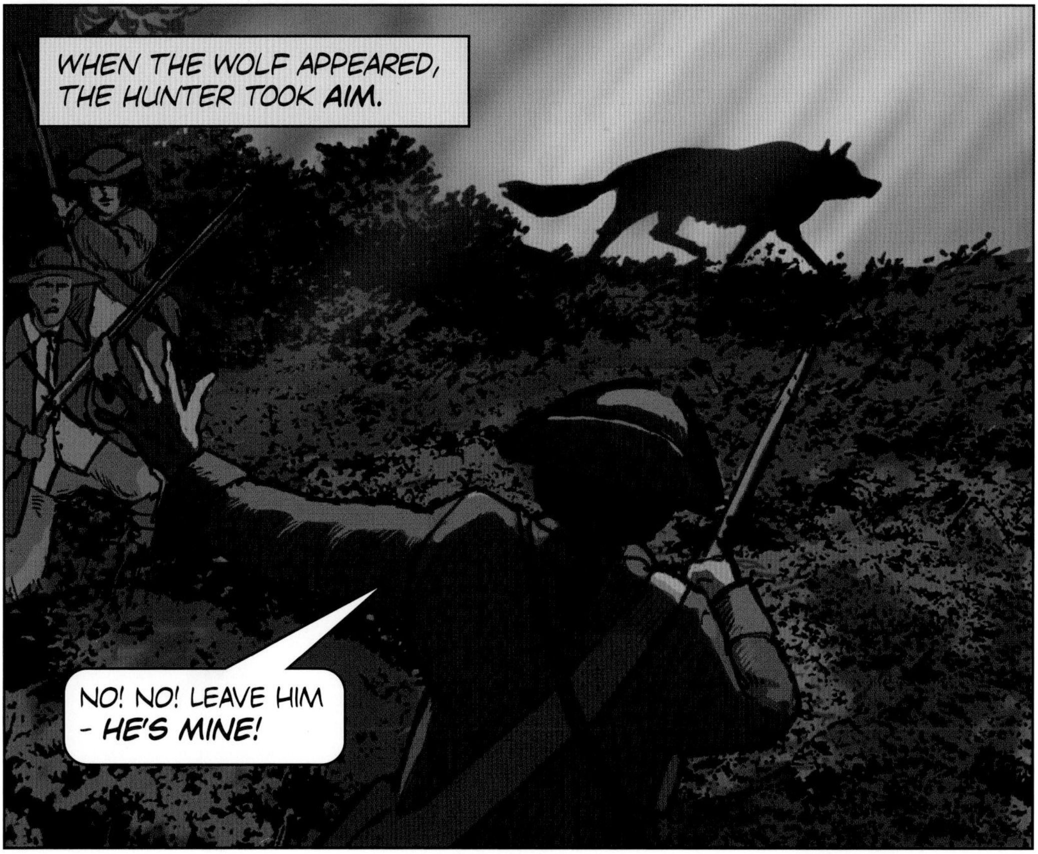
WHEN THE WOLF APPEARED, THE HUNTER TOOK **AIM.**
NO! NO! LEAVE HIM - ***HE'S MINE!***

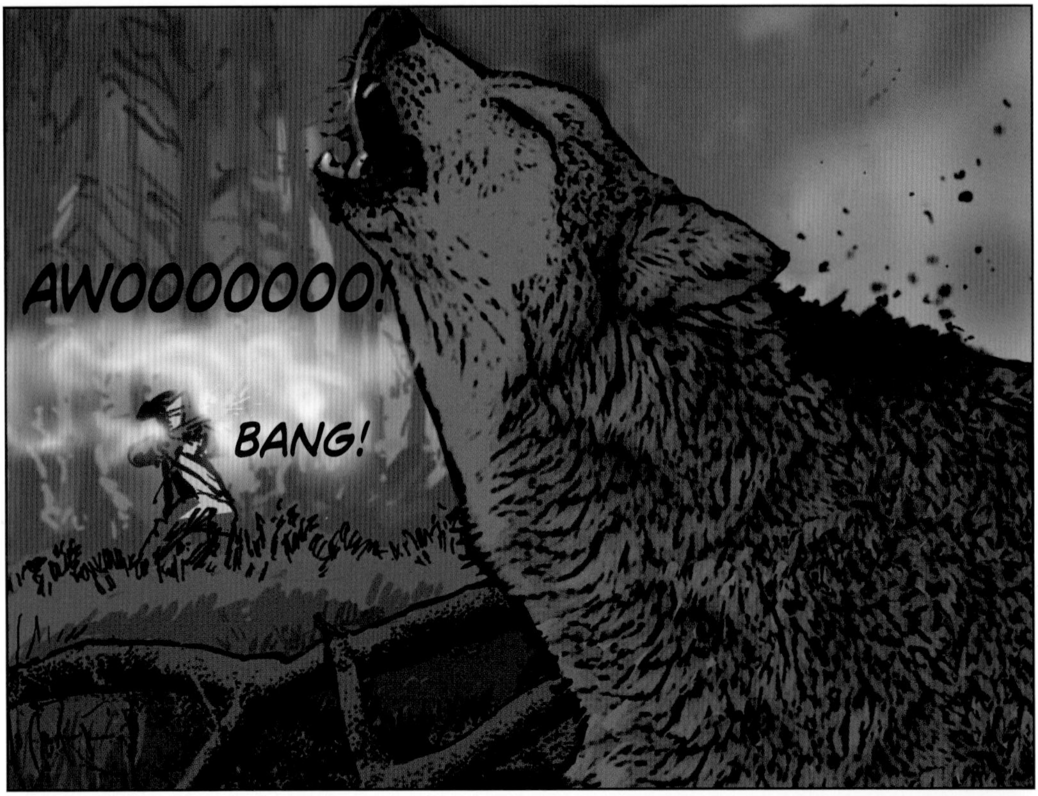
AWOOOOOOO!
BANG!

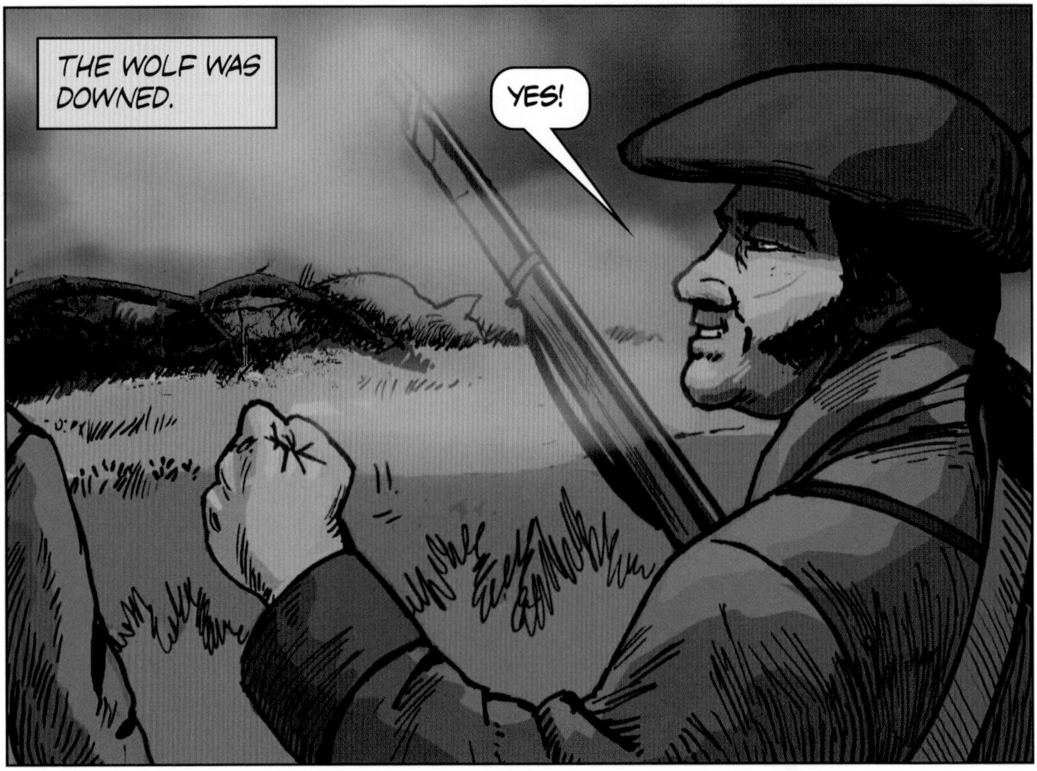
THE WOLF WAS DOWNED.
YES!

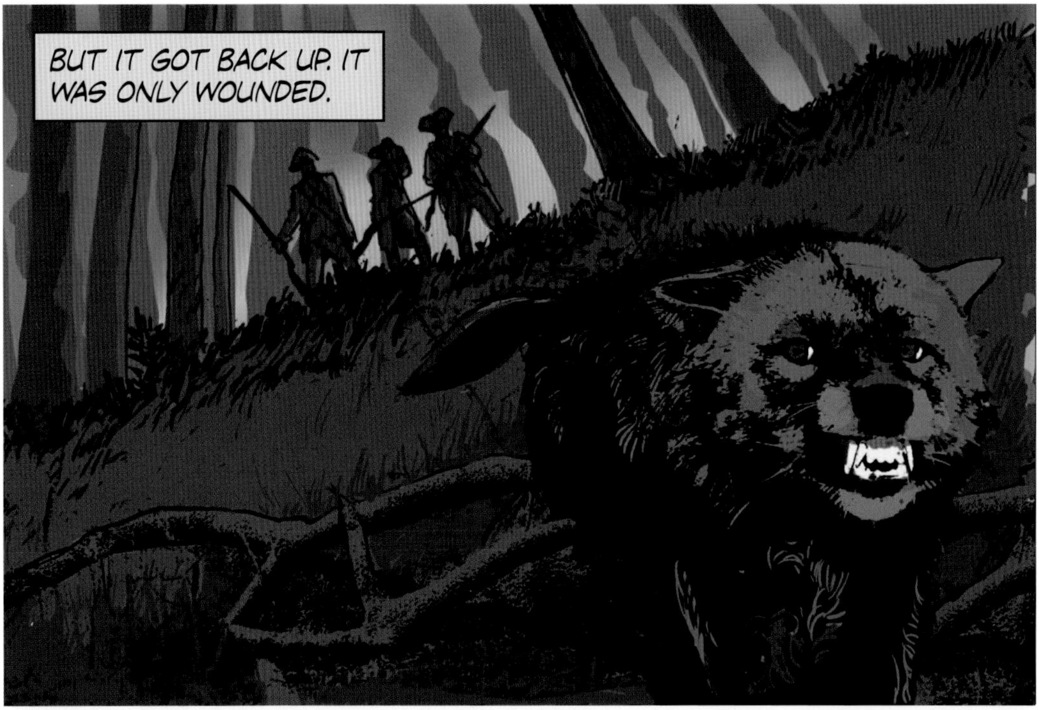
BUT IT GOT BACK UP. IT WAS ONLY WOUNDED.

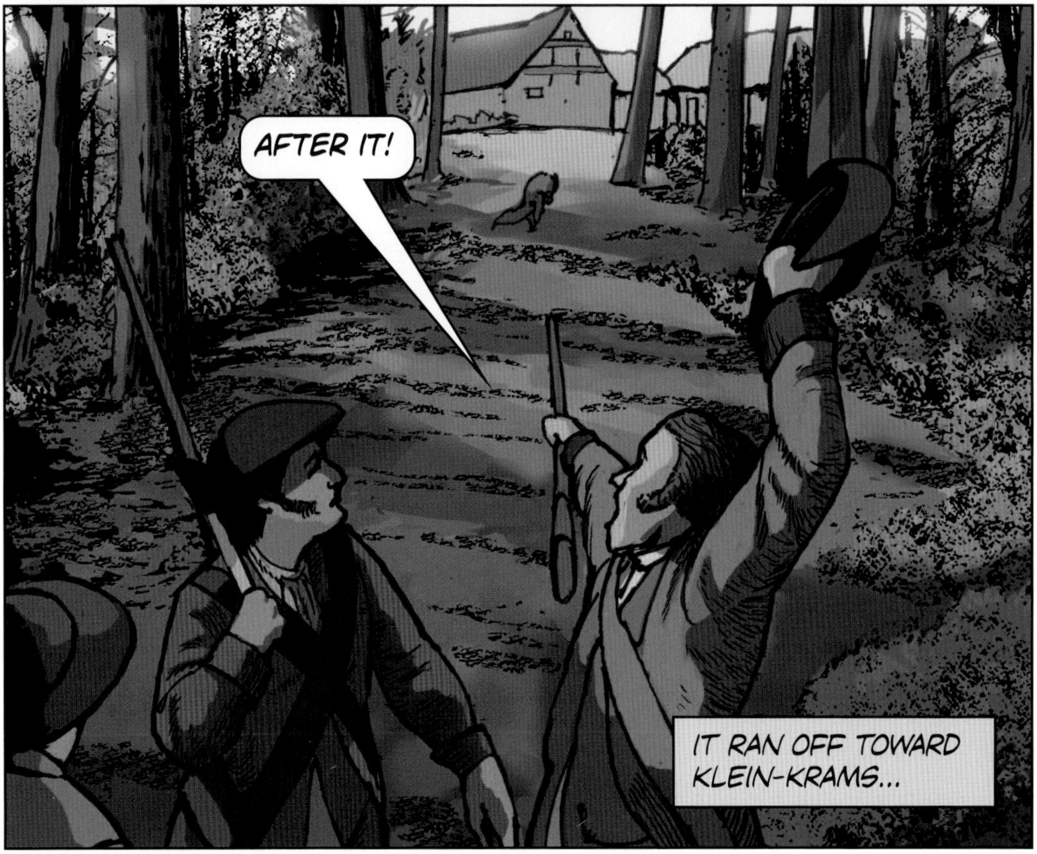
AFTER IT!
IT RAN OFF TOWARD KLEIN-KRAMS...

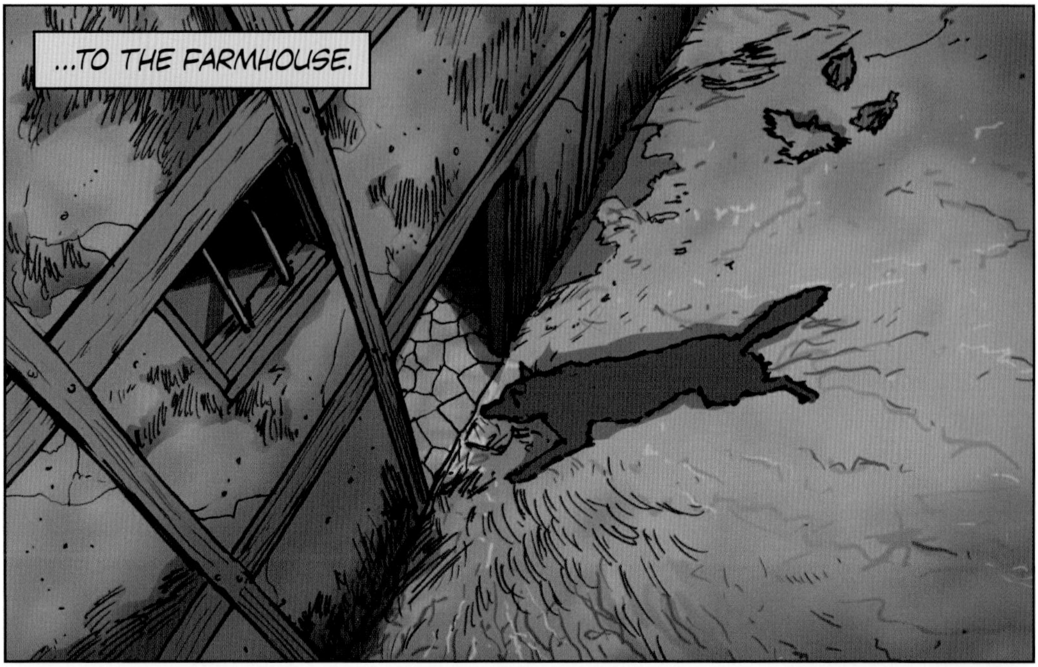
...TO THE FARMHOUSE.

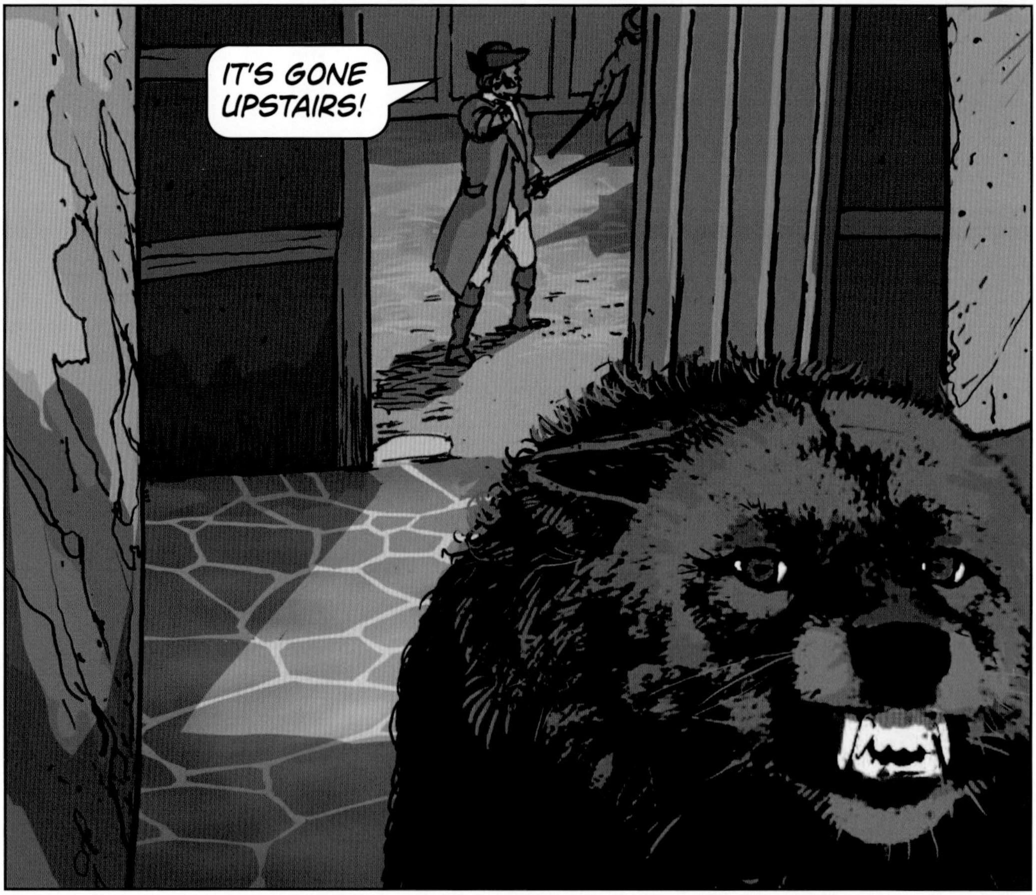
IT'S GONE UPSTAIRS!

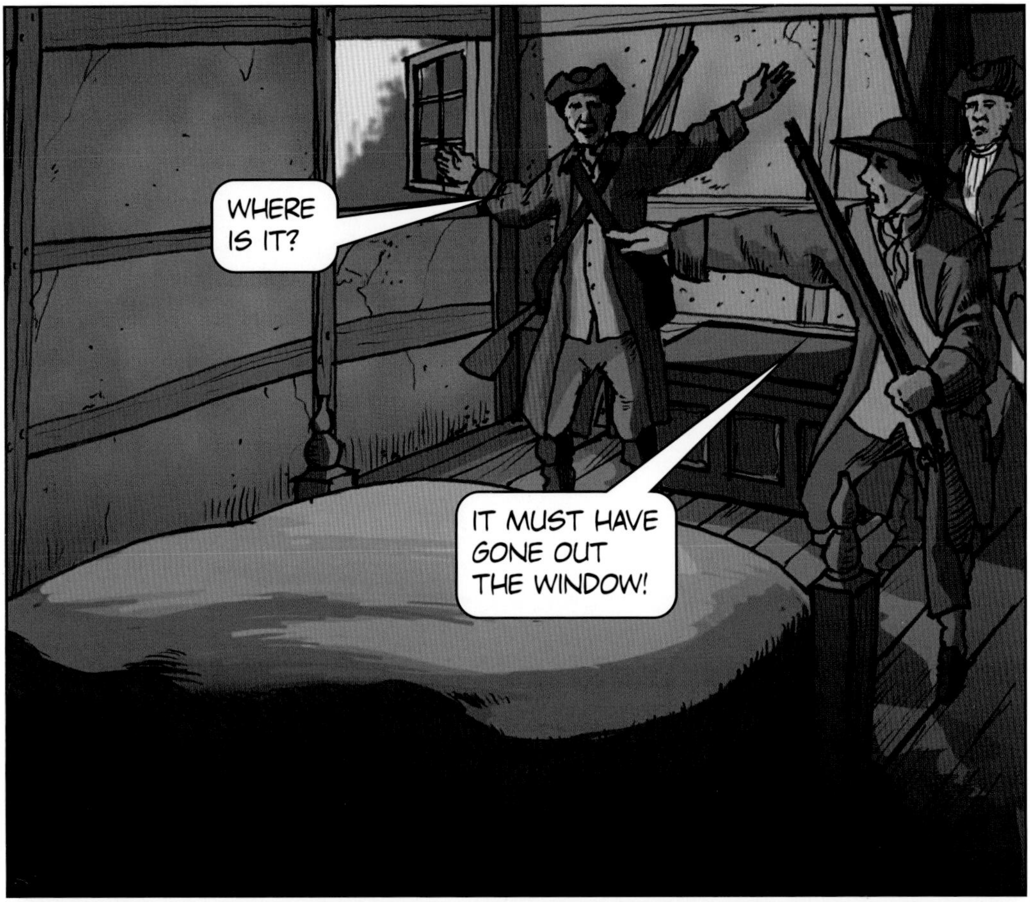
WHERE IS IT?
IT MUST HAVE GONE OUT THE WINDOW!

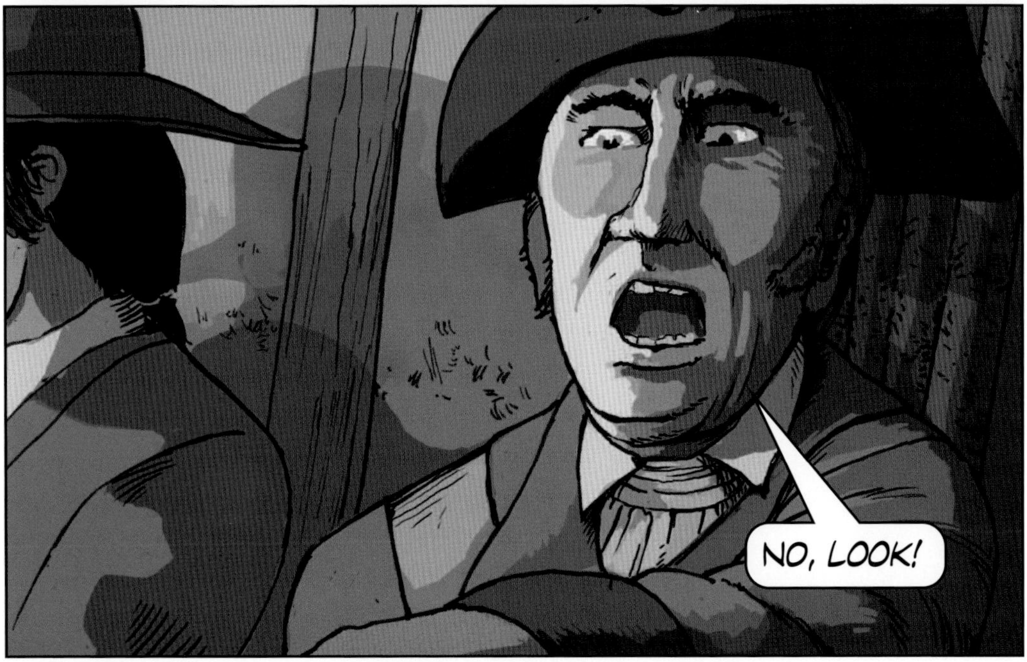
NO, LOOK!

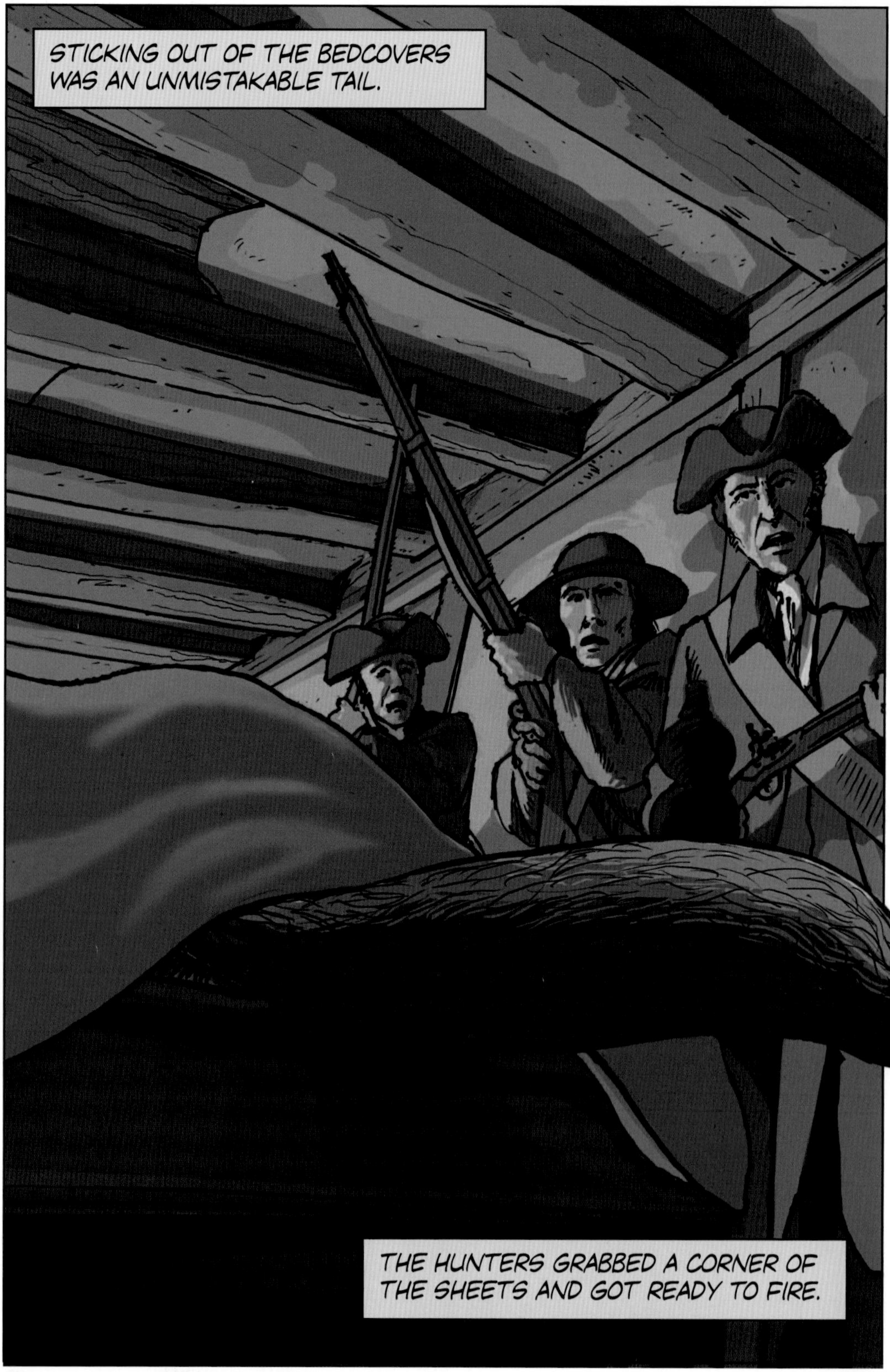
STICKING OUT OF THE BEDCOVERS WAS AN UNMISTAKABLE TAIL.
THE HUNTERS GRABBED A CORNER OF THE SHEETS AND GOT READY TO FIRE.

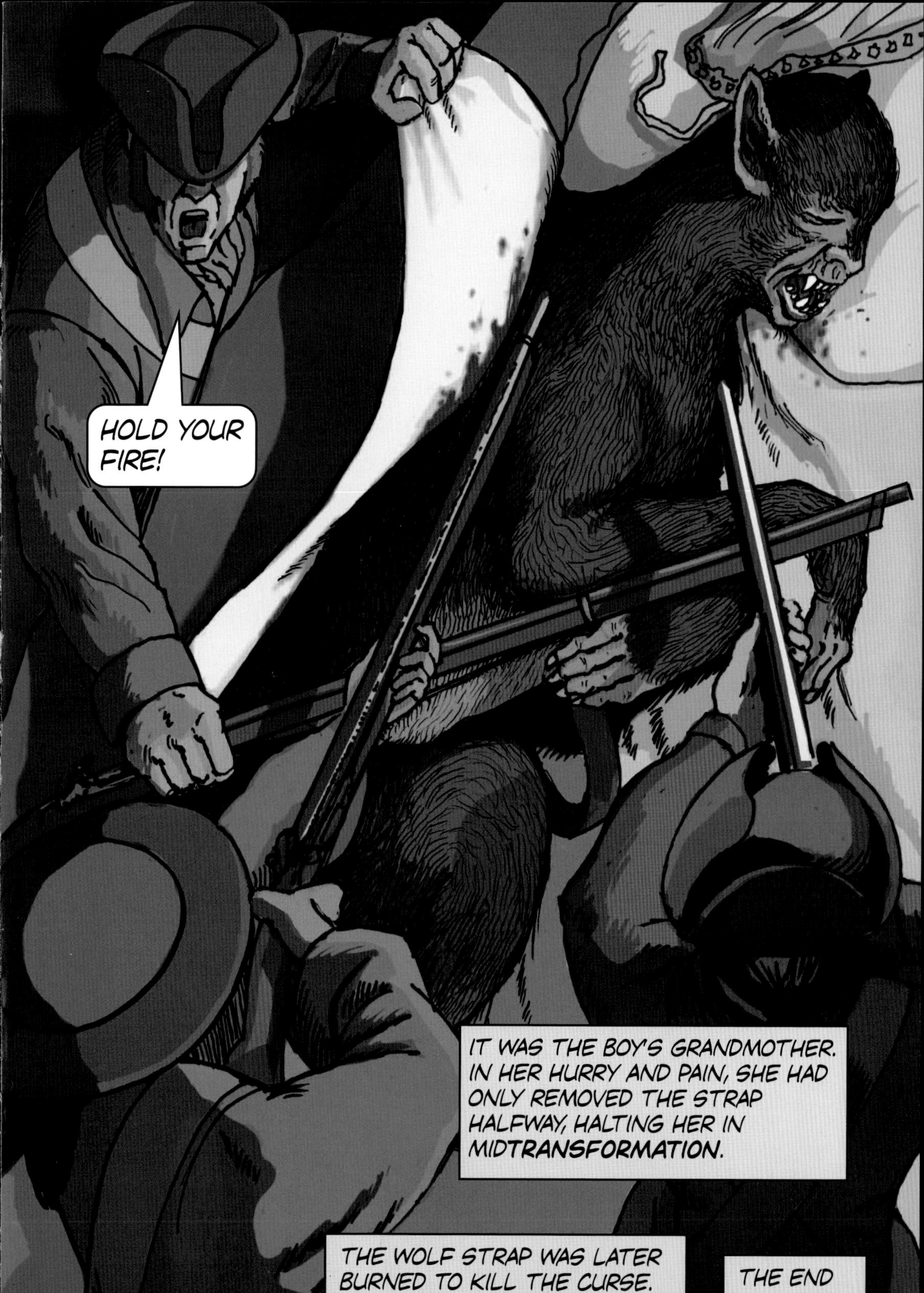
HOLD YOUR FIRE!
IT WAS THE BOY'S GRANDMOTHER. IN HER HURRY AND PAIN, SHE HAD ONLY REMOVED THE STRAP HALFWAY, HALTING HER IN MIDTRANSFORMATION.
THE WOLF STRAP WAS LATER BURNED TO KILL THE CURSE.
THE END

Other Werewolf Tales

Germany's enchanted forests play host to many other werewolf stories. Out-of-the-way regions of France, and even the United States, also offer up their own versions of the scariest and hairiest of mythical beasts...

Wolf of Magdeburg

A folktale from Saxony tells how, during a terrible winter, a wolf kidnaps the mayor's baby daughter. The beast is tracked to the forest by a wolf hunter called Breber. When he kills it, Breber discovers that the wolf is actually his wife.

The Werewolf's Curse

In 1736, a hunter in the wilds of Indiana fights for his life against a big black dog. When he wounds the dog, it magically transforms into... his best friend.

The Morbach Monster

A group of U.S. servicemen on a German air base mock the local werewolf legend, but then *something* breaks into the fog-bound munitions compound and gives them a scare.

The Beast of Gévaudan

A real-life series of gruesome killings takes place in the lonely mountains of central France. The shepherdesses and children seem to have been slain by a wolf. A hunt is mounted, and a huge wolf is caught. When the killings begin again, a werewolf is suspected.

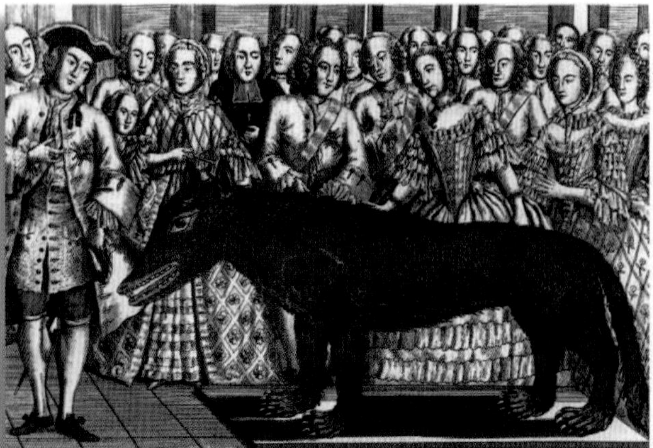

In 1765, the Beast of Gévaudan was caught and killed, but the killings went on. Was it a werewolf?

GLOSSARY

cult A group with unconventional beliefs that worships a being or ideas that often include the supernatural.

cunning Skill in deception.

curse An appeal to a supernatural power for harm to come to a specific person or group.

endurance The ability to withstand hardship or stress.

ferocious Extremely savage and fierce or cruel.

medieval Relating to the Middle Ages, a period of European history from the 5th to the 15th century.

mock To make fun of or treat with no respect.

munitions Military equipment, especially weapons and ammunition.

musket A smoothbore shoulder gun that was used from the 16th through the 18th centuries.

rampage To rush about in an angry or violent way.

shape-shifter A being that can alter its physical appearance, usually in order to trick someone else.

slain To have been killed violently.

INDEX